PRER
9/20

'90

Dear Parents:

Congratulations! Your child is taking the first steps on an exciting journey. The destination? Independent reading!

STEP INTO READING® will help your child get there. The program offers five steps to reading success. Each step includes fun stories and colorful art or photographs. In addition to original fiction and books with favorite characters, there are Step into Reading Non-Fiction Readers, Phonics Readers and Boxed Sets, Sticker Readers, and Comic Readers—a complete literacy program with something to interest every child.

Learning to Read, Step by Step!

Ready to Read   Preschool–Kindergarten
• big type and easy words • rhyme and rhythm • picture clues
For children who know the alphabet and are eager to begin reading.

Reading with Help   Preschool–Grade 1
• basic vocabulary • short sentences • simple stories
For children who recognize familiar words and sound out new words with help.

Reading on Your Own   Grades 1–3
• engaging characters • easy-to-follow plots • popular topics
For children who are ready to read on their own.

Reading Paragraphs   Grades 2–3
• challenging vocabulary • short paragraphs • exciting stories
For newly independent readers who read simple sentences with confidence.

Ready for Chapters   Grades 2–4
• chapters • longer paragraphs • full-color art
For children who want to take the plunge into chapter books but still like colorful pictures.

STEP INTO READING® is designed to give every child a successful reading experience. The grade levels are only guides; children will progress through the steps at their own speed, developing confidence in their reading.

Remember, a lifetime love of reading starts with a single step!

created by

Stephen Hillenburg

Visit us on the Web!
StepIntoReading.com
rhcbooks.com

Educators and librarians, for a variety of teaching tools, visit us at RHTeachersLibrarians.com

ISBN 978-0-593-12754-4 (trade) — ISBN 978-0-593-12755-1 (lib. bdg.)

Printed in the United States of America

10 9 8 7 6 5 4 3 2 1

HAPPY CAMPERS!

by David Lewman

based on the screenplay by Tim Hill

illustrated by Dave Aikins

Random House 🏠 New York

SpongeBob's mom and dad
take him to Camp Coral.

SpongeBob is

happy to go to camp!

SpongeBob hears

someone crying.

Who is it?

SpongeBob finds Patrick.
He asks Patrick why
he is crying.

Patrick says
he is homesick.
He cries harder!

SpongeBob says
maybe all Patrick needs
is a friend.

Patrick says
he does not have
any friends.

"Well, you have
one now!"
SpongeBob says.

"Who is it?"

Patrick asks.

"ME!" says SpongeBob.

The new friends
do lots of fun
things together.

They paddle
canoes on the lake.

They
catch jellyfish
and let them go.

They build
a huge
sand castle.

SpongeBob and Patrick
ride seahorses.

They swing

on long seaweed vines.

SpongeBob and Patrick perform together in the Camp Coral Talent Show.

They sing and dance!

They win a prize!

Mrs. Puff gives them the Campy Award!

SpongeBob and Patrick
will be best friends forever!